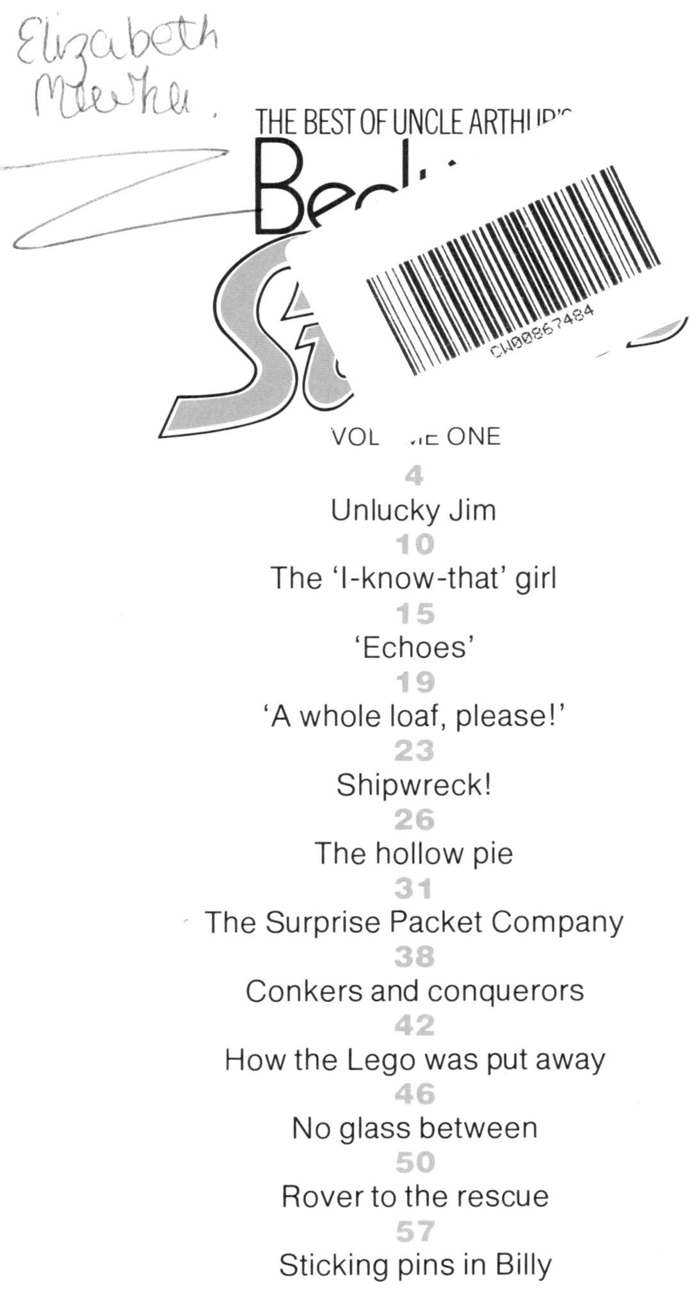

THE BEST OF UNCLE ARTHU

VOL ONE

Unlucky Jim

Jim thought he was the unluckiest boy that had ever been born. Everything seemed to go wrong for him. His outlook on life was particularly dark just now, for only a few minutes ago his one and only marble had rolled down a drain.

But quite apart from this calamity, he had much to make him feel blue. For one thing, he was shivering with cold. He should have had warm socks and underclothes to wear, but he hadn't any because there was not enough money to buy them. Father was out of work.

For another thing, he was hungry. It was some hours since lunch, and the bread and butter he had had then seemed to have gone clear down to the South Pole. As he trudged along the London streets with his hands in his pockets, he saw lots of other boys and girls going into beautiful homes for their tea, and he knew that he would have to climb up the dirty, narrow stairs of an East End tower block for the little bit of bread and jam that he would get.

Just then he passed a toyshop, all ablaze with lights and full of everything that might make a boy's heart glad. He stopped a moment and watched other boys and girls coming out with parcels under their arms. Jim jabbed his hand a little deeper down into his pocket and fingered his 2p once again, the only one he had left. How he wished he could buy something to take to his little sister, lying at home so sick!

'If I ain't the unluckiest feller that ever lived!' he said to himself.

But the next day his luck seemed to change. He was walking down the street near his home when a well-dressed lady stopped him.

'Is your name Jimmie Mackay?' she said.

'Yes, Miss', said Jimmie, surprised, and wondering what was going to happen.

'Well,' said the lady, 'we have your name on a list at our church, and we want you to come to a special Christmas party next week. Here is a ticket for you.'

'Great!' said Jimmie, not knowing what else to say. 'But what about Jean – she's my sister, yer know; she'll be better by then, p'rhaps; she ought to come too.'

'I'm afraid we can take only one from each family this time', said the lady kindly. 'We will try to take Jean next time.'

'Well, that's lucky and unlucky', said Jim to himself as the lady walked away. 'Lucky for me and unlucky for poor Jean.'

Then a bright idea occurred to him – perhaps he could let Jean go instead of him. He looked at his card. It read: 'Admit bearer – Jimmie Mackay – only.'

'Unlucky again!' murmured Jimmie.

So Jimmie went to the party. For most of the time he forgot all about his troubles. Everything was so different, so very wonderful. He had never had so much to eat in all his life.

After tea they all played games until it was time for the presents on the Christmas tree to be given away. What excitement there was then, especially as each child was to be allowed to choose just what he wanted most.

Jim could hardly sit still as he watched the other children going up in front of him. He felt as though he were on 'pins and needles'. He had seen such a wonderful toy train hanging on the tree – something he had wanted all his life – and how he did hope and hope and *hope* that no one would ask for it first!

At last – after what seemed hours – Jimmie's turn came.

'Jimmie Mackay!' called out the lady by the tree.

Jimmie jumped from his seat like a bullet from a gun. All he could see was the red engine; it was still there!

As he approached the lady, he noticed that she was the very one who had spoken to him in the street and given him his ticket for the party. Immediately a new idea came into his mind.

'And what would you like to have, Jimmie?' asked the lady. 'You may have any one thing you like from the tree.'

What an offer! Jimmie could scarcely take it in.

He stood and gazed up at the sparkling, heavily-laden tree. Once more his eye caught sight of the engine.

'Most of all,' he said, looking up at the lady, 'I

would like that red engine; but if you don't mind, I will take that fairy doll over there.'

Tears filled his eyes as he said it, but he kept his face straight.

Somehow the lady seemed to understand, and without a word she brought Jimmie the doll. As he went away, she squeezed his hand, and bending down, whispered, 'God bless you, Jimmie.'

But the other children did not understand at all. There was a great outburst of noise. With whoops and yells they told the world that Jimmie had chosen a doll. Some of the boys called out 'Sissy!' and others, with a laugh, 'Imagine a boy taking a doll!' And the little girls said, 'That was just the doll we wanted!'

Jimmie blushed. He couldn't help it. Finally he became so uncomfortable that he put on his coat and went out, with the doll under his arm.

All the way home he thought about the bad luck that seemed to have followed him that evening. First, he had lost his train engine, and secondly he had been laughed at by the whole crowd of children.

'If I'm not the unluckiest feller –' he began. Then he felt the doll under his arm. At once his thoughts brightened and his step quickened.

A few minutes later, he was up in the little dark bedroom where Jean lay sick in bed.

'I'm so glad you've come!' said Jean. 'It's so

lonely here all by myself. What have you got there?' she asked, sitting up in bed and peering at the doll with eager eyes. 'Is that for me? Oh, Jimmie, Jimmie, you *are* a dear!'

Jimmie forgot all about his bad luck. A thrill of joy went through him as he saw his sister's delight. How glad he was that he had chosen the doll and not the engine!

Just then there was a knock at the door. It was the lady from the party.

'What –' began Jimmie.

'I've come to say how sorry I am that the children were so unkind to you this evening', interrupted the lady. 'They are sorry too, now. I told them why you chose the doll. And they asked me to bring you something for yourself. Here it is. Now I must go, as it is getting late. Good night' – and she was gone.

Jimmie gasped, and then opened the parcel.

It was the red engine!

Then he danced a jig around Jean's bed, chuckling to himself, and saying:

'If I ain't the luckiest feller that ever lived!'

The 'I-know-that' girl

I don't know whether you know her or not. Perhaps you do. Anyway you probably know someone like her. This little girl that I know used to think that she knew everything, and yet she was only 8 years old. When her daddy told her anything she would say, 'I know that.' Or if Mummy pointed out something new in a shop window, she would say, 'Oh, I have seen that before.' She just wouldn't admit that there was anything she didn't know. It was quite impossible to surprise her with anything. If you took her to town and bought her a new umbrella for her birthday and then asked her afterwards if she was pleased with it, she would say, 'Well, I thought I was going to get an umbrella, anyway.'

Of course nobody liked to take her anywhere. If people came to her house and wanted to give the children a treat, they would whisper to her daddy, 'I think we will only take the boys this time.' Of course they were too polite to say what they thought of the little girl, but Daddy knew what was the matter.

One day there was great excitement in the home of Miss 'I-Know-That'. Daddy had announced that he was going to take her to London all by herself. How pleased she was! And to think that she was the only one going!

On the way in the train her daddy tried to make the journey interesting. He tried hard not to read his newspaper, and kept pointing out all the things that most little girls would be glad to see.

'I know that', she said. 'I remember seeing that before.'

At last Daddy got a bit tired, and changed the subject.

'Supposing', he said, 'that you were to lose me in London. What would you do?'

'Oh, go home', she said, as though she didn't care.

'But how?' asked Daddy.

'Oh, just walk to the station and get on the train.'

'But how would you know the way?'

'Oh, well – er – that's easy; I know that.'

An hour later they were down in Trafalgar Square, gazing up at Lord Nelson standing there so cold and lonely on the top of his tall pillar.

There were crowds of people hurrying about, but the little girl didn't seem to notice them. She was too interested in the big stone lions and the man at the top of the pillar. She did not like to admit that this was something new to her, but at last she turned around to ask Daddy all about it.

'Why', she asked, 'is that man with one arm standing up there on top of that pole?'

She stopped and looked round for Daddy – but there was no Daddy to be seen.

'Daddy!'

No answer.

'Daddeeeeee!'

Still no reply. Daddy had gone, and she was alone.

Now she thought of what she had said about knowing the way home. She looked at the hundreds of people who were going past her in all directions, up at the great buildings, out over the streets where buses and cars were rushing by, and at last the truth came to her that she really didn't know anything at all about the way home. There were hundreds of buses, how could she tell which one to take? She didn't even know the name of the railway station.

Then she began to cry. For a little while nobody seemed to take any notice of her. The people were all in too much of a hurry. But after a little while a policeman came across the road and, bending down, asked her very kindly what was the matter.

'I'm lost!' she sobbed.

'Lost! Why, who were you with?' asked the policeman.

'My daddy, and he's gone.'

'Gone where?'

'I don't know. Boo-hoo-hoo!'

'Where do you live?'

'I don't know. Boo-hoo-hoo!'

'Well, come along with me, then.'

'No, I don't want to go to the police station! Boo-hoo-hoo-hoo!'

'Well, I can't leave you here. I'm afraid you'll have to come with me, then we'll find your daddy.'

So the policeman and little Miss 'I-Know-That' walked off towards the police station, the little girl quietly sobbing as she trotted along at his side.

They had not gone far when a familiar voice from behind called out, 'Girlie!'

Forgetting all about the policeman and her troubles, she turned round and jumped into her daddy's arms.

'Oh, I'm so glad you've come!' she said, 'I thought I was lost.'

They had a big hug right there in Trafalgar Square. When she wasn't looking, Daddy winked at the policeman, and the policeman winked at Daddy.

'You see,' said Daddy, 'I only wanted to see whether you really did know the way home as you said you did.'

And ever after that when she was tempted to say, 'I know that', she thought of the policeman and Trafalgar Square – and didn't say it.

'Echoes'

Mother and 7-year-old Marie were on their way into town from their little bungalow in the country. On the way they passed by a group of boys in a field, who were making all sorts of strange noises.

'What are those boys doing?' asked Marie.

'I don't know', said Mother, 'let's go and see.'

'Hal-lo! Yoo-hoo! Pe-ter! Yoo-hoo!' yelled the boys.

Then they stopped a moment and listened.

Faintly but distinctly came back the same sounds:

'Hal-lo! Yoo-hoo! Pe-ter! Yoo-hoo!'

'I know now,' said Mother, 'they are listening for the echo.'

'What's an echo?' asked Marie.

'A repeated sound', said Mother. 'The noises those boys are making reach that high wall at the other side of the field, and bounce back to them again. It seems as though the wall is speaking to them, but it only repeats exactly what they say to it.'

'Would the wall speak to me?' asked Marie.

'Oh, yes. You can try if you like.'

So Marie went over to where the boys were standing, and they waited until she called. She could not think of anything to shout except, 'Mummy!'

There was a brief silence, then 'Mummy!' came back from the wall.

'Mummy,' said Marie, 'someone must want you over there.'

'Oh, no,' said Mother, with a smile. 'That was only the wall repeating what you said.'

On the way to town and back Marie could think of nothing else but the echo she had heard. She was very pleased when Mother told her that she would be able to listen to an echo at home. She decided to try it as soon as they were indoors.

So when they reached home Marie went into every room, calling, 'Mummy!', and listening for the echo. But there was no reply. She was so disappointed.

'Mummy,' she said, running into the kitchen, 'I thought you said I should hear an echo indoors.'

'Yes, dear, and most likely you will hear it at dinnertime.'

'It's nearly that now', said Marie.

'Yes,' said Mother, 'Bring Kevin in out of the garden and put him in his chair.'

In a few minutes dinner was served.

'I don't want any of those horrid potatoes', said Marie.

'I don't want any of those horrid 'tatoes', repeated Kevin.

Mother said nothing, but put out the potatoes. Then she prepared to serve the cabbage.

'Mummy, I hate cabbage', exclaimed Marie.

'Mummy, I hate cabbit!' said Kevin.

But Mother put out the cabbage, and the children ate it; they had to, with Mummy looking so stern.

When it came to pudding time, Marie had some more comments to make.

'Only custard for me; you know I don't like rhubarb.'

'Only cus'ard for me; you know I don't like woobarb', said Kevin.

Then Marie smiled, and Mother smiled too.

'I think I heard an echo', said Mother.

'So did I', said Marie, with a blush and a giggle. Just then it had dawned upon Marie that little Kevin was repeating nearly everything she said, and particularly the naughty things. All of a sudden she felt very grown up. She seemed to see herself as Kevin's schoolteacher.

'I think', she said, 'that I had better give him only good words to echo after this.'

And Mother was so pleased that she walked round the table and gave Marie a great big kiss. And though Mother did not say anything, you could see she was pleased and very happy.

'A whole loaf, please!'

A long time ago awful things began to happen in Russia. First the royal family were shot, then there was much suffering among the people. Many thousands starved to death. Thousands of the poor became poorer and some became beggars. It was hard for children to understand, for the change came so suddenly on them all. I think many of them must have 'cried their eyes out' many times.

There was one family that I know about that had a very hard time. Their Father had been killed, Mother had died, and Grandma was left with three children. Once they had lived in a beautiful home, and their table had always been spread with plenty of good things to eat. Now they were living in a hut. Grandma was knitting hard all day to try to earn enough to keep the children alive. But when she had finished her knitting it was very difficult to swap it for food. There was so little food to be found anywhere.

One day the last morsel had been eaten. After a crust of bread each for the midday meal, there was not a crumb left in the house. Grandma was very, very sad, but she tried not to let the children see her worry. She called them around her, told them what was the matter, and then they knelt down to pray. She felt that she had run out of all the things she could do to help, and that unless Jesus helped them they would surely die of starvation like the other poor people around them.

So they prayed. What a prayer meeting that was – just Grandma and the three children; but they all prayed as only very hungry people can.

I don't know what they all said, but the little girl's prayer was like this:

'Dear Jesus, please send us something for tea; not just a crust, but a whole loaf, please.'

They had not seen a whole loaf for a long time, and it was like asking for a birthday cake for an ordinary meal.

Teatime came, but still there was no food. How those children must have longed for something to eat!

'You haven't sharpened the breadknife yet', said the little girl to Grandma, still fully believing that her prayer would be answered.

So Grandma sharpened the knife, according to Russian custom.

The evening passed. Cold and hungry, the children were about to go to bed when there was a knock at the door.

A man stood outside, covered with snow. He had walked nearly twenty miles that day. Grandma recognized him as an old friend of the family, and welcomed him in.

'What has brought you here tonight?' she asked.

'About noon today something impressed me that you were in great need and that I must come to you at once.'

Then turning to the children he said, 'And you will never guess what I have brought with me.'

'I can', said the little girl.

'What is it, then?' asked the gentleman.

'It's a whole big loaf', said the little girl.

'And that's just what it is!' said the friend, opening his overcoat and taking out the loaf. 'And how did you know?'

Then they told him how they had prayed that Jesus would send them not a crust, but a whole loaf, and together they went down on their knees and thanked Jesus for His wonderful care for those who believe in Him.

And though it was only a loaf and no butter on it, what a wonderful supper they had that night!

Shipwreck!

'Help! We are sinking!'

Far out in the great Pacific Ocean a little ship called the *Sterling*, was fighting for life amid a terrible storm. Waves mountains high were sweeping over her. Water was pouring into her hold, and it seemed impossible to keep the ship afloat much longer.

Going to his radio cabin, the captain sent out his call for help. Perhaps it would be heard by someone. There was little hope, for the ship was hundreds of miles from land and, for all the captain knew, there might be no other ships near enough to hear the call.

The storm grew worse, and the brave sailors realized that the end was near. Again the call went out, Help!

Hundreds of miles away the Australian battleship *Melbourne* was steaming towards home. Suddenly through the air came the desperate call of the *Sterling*. Immediately the great battleship changed her course and, at full speed, steamed towards the sinking ship.

Hours passed. Meanwhile the *Sterling*, battered by the mighty waves, was rapidly sinking. Would the *Melbourne* reach her in time?

It seemed impossible. Going to the radio cabin

again, the captain sent out this message:

'Can't last another hour. Water-logged. Sea sweeping right over us. Clearing boats, but impossible to live in this sea. Farewell!'

Then back from the captain of the *Melbourne* came this stirring and beautiful message:

'WE ARE CERTAIN TO REACH YOU: KEEP GOOD HEART.'

The captain of the *Melbourne* kept his word. Just before the *Sterling* sank, the great battleship came alongside and, by gallant efforts, transferred the crew of the wrecked ship across the boiling sea to safety.

Sometimes boys and girls are just like the ship *Sterling*. Maybe you know some of them. They want to be good, and they struggle with what they know to be wrong. But storms of temptation come, and it seems impossible to resist them.

At such times as these there is only one thing to do. That is to radio for help: 'Sinking, can't last another hour!'

Jesus will hear. He understands our thoughts. (Read Psalm 139:2.) Instantly He will reply: 'I am certain to reach you. Keep good heart.'

There is no need to 'go under', no need to give way to wrong. Jesus will save. But be sure to avoid shipwreck by calling Him in time.

The hollow pie

Robert had a bad habit of always taking the biggest and best of everything for himself.

His brothers, Charlie and Tim, would call him all sorts of names for doing it, but it didn't seem to make any difference.

Mother was upset about it too, especially as Robert, when invited out to parties, always disgraced the family with his greediness. What could be done? Mother put on her thinking cap and talked the matter over with Aunty who lived in the next street.

A few days later the boys were delighted to receive an invitation to tea from their aunty. Remembering all the good things they had enjoyed there before, they looked forward to the day of the party with much excitement.

At last the day came and tea-time arrived – Robert had been waiting for this!

The table was piled with good things, cakes, fruit, jellies, pies, chocolates and the rest.

Robert's eyes roamed around the wonderful spread of tasty things. 'Oh!' he thought, 'if only I could sit here all by myself!'

Then he spied a beautiful pear on the fruit dish. It was one of the biggest he had ever seen. There and then he decided to have it some time during the evening. He also looked around at the other things and made up his mind which of them he would choose when the plates were passed round.

When all the visitors had been given their places around the table, tea began. Of course, they all started with sandwiches in the usual way. Robert, however, soon got tired of them. He wanted that big pie he could see on a plate at the other side of the table. Would he get it in time, or would Charlie?

The pies were passed round. Charlie and Tim took small ones, and opened them. 'What wonderful fillings they've got!' thought Robert. 'Now, if I can get that big one . . .'

Robert's turn came. The biggest pie was still there, and of course he took it.

But a disappointment awaited him. As he cut through the top, the whole pie collapsed. It was hollow!

Poor Robert! Tears filled his eyes, but as no one seemed to notice what had happened he ate the crust as bravely as he could, and said nothing.

The cakes were passed around. Robert felt it was quite all right to take the biggest again, seeing that there had been nothing in his pie.

But something was wrong with his cake. It looked fine on the outside, but the centre was bitter. What could be the matter? thought Robert. Aunty was such a good cook. And then, too, the others didn't seem to be having any trouble at all. It wasn't fair, thought Robert, but he didn't dare say anything for fear the others would laugh at him.

Now came the fruit. How thankful Robert was that the plate was passed down his side of the table first! He felt sure Charlie was after that big pear. Anyhow, he would get it first.

The plate reached Robert and he put his hand into the middle of the pile of fruit. Oranges and apples scattered in all directions over the tablecloth, but Robert got his pear.

His teeth were soon busy, but oh, dear! something seemed to be the matter again. Taking his knife Robert cut the pear in two. To his utter disgust he found the centre was bad.

Still nobody seemed to notice Robert's problem, and no one passed him anything to make up for his misfortunes. The others all seemed to be enjoying themselves to the full.

The chocolates came next, and by this time Robert was getting desperate. 'I shall have to make up for lost time by taking those two big ones in the centre', he said to himself, as he removed the two best-looking chocolates from the plate.

'Ugh!' said Robert, groaning inwardly, and blushing all over with disappointment. 'What a horrible taste!' Swallowing one with difficulty he tried the other 'to take the taste away', only to find it was worse.

On the way home Charlie remarked to Robert

about the smashing tea they had had.

'Smashing what?' said Robert.

'I thought you were not enjoying yourself', said Charlie. 'You looked uncomfortable. What was the matter?'

'Matter?' said Robert, 'Everything I took was bad, even though I did take what looked best every time.'

'Maybe that was the cause of the trouble, Robert', said Charlie, smiling. 'I think if I were you I would leave the biggest and best-looking things for somebody else next time.'

That night Robert stayed awake quite a long time. There were two reasons. One was a pain under his pyjama jacket and the other was the advice Charlie had given him. He put two and two together and at last decided that the best and safest course for him would be to follow Charlie's suggestion in the future.

The Surprise Packet Company

'I wish I could be a pirate!' said Wilfred. 'Everything is so dull, and I want to do something exciting.'

'Yes', said Gwen, 'let's find something to do.'

It was holiday time. School had been closed for about ten days, and the children were getting tired of their games. They wanted something new.

'Of course, we can't be pirates,' said Gwen, 'because we should soon be taken to the police station.'

'Of course,' said Wilfred, 'but can't we think of something?'

'Let's think.'

So they thought and thought. Neither of them spoke for several minutes. Then Wilfred jumped to his feet.

'I've got it!' he cried. 'Let's call ourselves the "Surprise Packet Company". 'I'll be the manager, and you – well, you can be the secretary.'

'All right, Wilf,' said Gwen, willing to do anything her big brother suggested, 'but what shall we do?'

'Do? Give people surprises.'

'What sort?'

'Oh, good ones, of course', said Wilfred. 'We'll

find people who need things done for them and then make them wonder how the things happened. I think we'll get lots of fun out of it.'

'So do I', said Gwen; 'what shall we do first? Let's start soon.'

'All right. I'll make a list of things and then we can decide which to start with.'

Wilfred found a pencil and paper, and made his list.

'Now, mind,' he said solemnly, 'don't you go and tell anybody about what we are planning to do. It's just a secret between us two.'

'Of course,' said Gwen, 'as if I would tell!'

That same afternoon when mother returned from town she just dropped into an armchair and stared. What a transformation! After dinner she had gone out hurriedly, leaving all the dirty dishes beside the sink. Now they had disappeared. The kitchen had been tidied up, everything was in its place, and the table was all set for tea. The empty coal-scuttle had been filled, and, yes, even the windows had been cleaned!

All was quiet and still. Nobody was about. What kind person could have done all this?

Wilfred and Gwen came in from the garden. Mother asked them if aunty had called during the afternoon. Wilfred said No, he didn't think so, but it did look as though someone had been busy.

'Well,' said Mother, 'isn't it lovely! I haven't any more work to do today, and I can have such a nice quiet rest this evening! I wonder who did it all?'

Mother opened a letter she had found on the mat when coming in. It read:

'The "Surprise Packet Company" called this afternoon on a little matter of business.'

'I wonder what that means?' said Mother.

'I wonder', said Wilfred.

'Let's have tea', said Gwen.

And they did.

Next morning two children might have been seen going down the street leading to the little home of Mrs. O'Higgins, a poor, bed-ridden old lady for whom nobody seemed to care.

The boy, who was holding something carefully in his right hand, knocked gently on the door. There was no answer. The boy peeped through the window. Mrs. O'Higgins was fast asleep. Quietly opening the door, the boy walked in, followed by his sister. Tiptoeing across the room the boy placed the parcel he was carrying on the table beside the bed and went out. The little girl was so excited that she fell over the doorstep.

'Gwen, be careful!' said the boy.

The noise had awakened the old lady.

'Who is that?' she called.

But the door was shut, and the two children were

scampering away as fast as their legs would carry them.

Mrs. O'Higgins picked up the parcel. It contained three eggs.

'What a mercy!' she said to herself. 'But who sent them?'

Looking at the wrapper she read: 'With love from the "Surprise Packet Company".'

Frank Morley, a school friend of Wilfred's, was ill with mumps. Of course he had to stay indoors and was very miserable. From his bed he could just look out over a small patch of garden, surrounded by a high brick wall.

One afternoon he was gazing vacantly out of the window when all of a sudden he saw a square box topple over the garden wall and slide down to the ground, held by a piece of strong string.

'Mother, quick!' he called. 'Can you see what that is in the garden?'

Mother, all surprised, fetched the parcel which was addressed to Frank and he opened it. Inside were four smaller parcels. One was labelled, 'Open on Monday'; the second, 'Open Wednesday'; the third, 'Open Friday'; and the fourth, 'Open Sunday'.

As it was Monday, Frank opened the first parcel. It was a box of paints. Just what he had been longing for! Frank thought that he had seen the box before, but didn't know where. Inside the box were the words:

'With best wishes from the "Surprise Packet Company".'

'Whatever is that?' asked Frank.

Nobody knew.

On one occasion the 'Surprise Packet Company' was caught.

Wilfred and Gwen were paying a second visit to Mrs. O'Higgins.

This time they had taken with them some flowers as well as eggs. As quiet as mice they crept in, placed their gifts on the table, and left.

The children were so anxious to get in and out without waking the old lady that they did not notice a gentleman sitting quietly in the next room. It was the doctor.

No sooner had the door closed behind the children than he went across to the table, picked up the parcel and read the note:

'With love from the "Surprise Packet Company".'

'So this explains what the old lady has been talking about!' he thought. 'And now I can understand what Frank Morley told me yesterday.'

And this explains too, how it came about that a few days later a letter arrived at the home of

Wilfred and Gwen addressed to the 'Surprise Packet Company' and containing an invitation to tea at Dr. Brown's.

It was a wonderful tea that the children had at the doctor's and there were two surprise packets there that made up for all that they had given away.

Of course the children could not understand how the doctor had come to know about their secret, and he wouldn't say a word. It was all a delightful mystery. Wilfred and Gwen were as happy as children could be. Wilfred said that it was much better than being pirates!

Conkers and conquerors

Paul loved playing conkers. In a box at home he had a hundred and fifty-two. He knew, for he had counted them lots of times.

On his way to school he passed a horse chestnut tree, and every time he went by, Paul picked up all the conkers he could find to add to his collection at home.

One of his conkers was a real veteran. He had kept it for two years, and it was as hard as iron. It had won eighty-five battles, and had smashed all opponents. Paul was proud of it and believed that it would never be beaten.

One fine autumn afternoon Paul was at school with his pockets and his mind full of conkers. While teacher was writing on the board, Paul was challenging all the boys within whispering distance to a battle with his veteran conker.

Just then someone came to the classroom door and the teacher was called away.

'Get on with your lesson', he said to the boys as he went out. But they were not listening.

Hardly had the door closed behind him than out from a dozen pockets came as many conkers, all on strings and ready for active service.

Whack, whack, crack! Paul's veteran was more than a match for the others, and pieces of conker

were soon flying all over the classroom.

'Look out!' cried someone. Conkers and strings disappeared, a dive was made for the pieces, and then all pretended to be reading their books.

Teacher returned and looked suspiciously around. Then he saw something on the floor. He knew perfectly well what it meant.

'Has any boy been playing with horse chestnuts while I have been out?' he asked.

There was an awful silence.

Paul was fighting a battle. Should he own up? If he did, he would probably lose his much-prized veteran conker, and his victories over the other boys would be ended. If he didn't, well, would it matter anyway?

Teacher had once been a boy himself, and knew what was going on at that moment in some boy's mind. Without saying a word he went to the blackboard and wrote:

Conker
Conquer
Conqueror

Then, turning round, he said, 'Is there any boy here who is going to let himself be beaten by a horse chestnut?'

It was too much for Paul. It came home to him that the eighty-five battles of his veteran conker were as nothing compared with this one fight with himself.

He rose to his feet and, blushing to the roots of his hair, said, 'I played while you were out, sir.'

'Bring me your conker.'

Paul sadly obeyed, handing over his veteran, string and all.

'Thank you', said the teacher. 'But the game of conkers cannot be played by one person. Others have been playing too, but have not had the courage to own up.'

That night Paul told his mother what had happened. Mother understood.

'I would rather have my boy an honest, truthful conqueror,' she told him, 'than have all the conkers in the world.'

And Paul agreed.

How the Lego was put away

'Bedtime!' called Mummy. 'Put the Lego away.'

'No! No! No!' cried the children in a chorus of disapproval.

'Don't want to go to bed', said Jimmie, the youngest.

'It's so early', said Gerald; 'I'm not tired.'

'And I'm not going to put the Lego away,' said Sheila, 'because I didn't get it out.'

'And I didn't', said Gerald.

'And I didn't', repeated Jimmie.

'But you can't leave the dining room like this', said Mummy. 'Daddy will be coming home soon, and he always likes to see the place tidy.'

'Well, I'm not going to put the things away', said Gerald. 'That's Sheila's job.'

'It's not my job, Mummy. I think Gerald's mean; he should do it himself.'

'I can't do it', said Jimmie with a sigh. 'I'm too tired.'

'Well,' said Mummy, 'somebody must do it; and I will give you just five minutes to decide. If the Lego is not away then – well, you know what will happen.'

So Mummy went into the kitchen and closed the

door behind her. The three children sat on the floor and looked at the pile of Lego. Then they scowled at one another.

'You should put them away', said Sheila to Gerald. 'You're mean.'

'So are you. I shan't do it, so there', and Gerald pulled his feet up under him and locked his hands over his knees. He looked cross.

Slowly the minutes ticked away.

'Mummy will be here in two minutes, and then you'll catch it', said Sheila.

'So will you.'

'But it's your job', insisted Sheila.

'It isn't; it's yours', replied Gerald.

Sheila looked at the clock.

'There's only another minute', she said; 'and you know Mummy always does what she says.'

'Well, put the things away, then.'

'I won't; it's your job.'

'It isn't; it's yours.'

'I tell you what', interrupted little Jimmie. 'Let's each put some away, one after the other; and I'll start.'

'Not a bad idea, Jimmie', said Gerald.

So Jimmie brought the box and put in the first handful. Sheila followed with another, and then Gerald. Soon they were trying to see who could pick up the Lego quickest. Before the last minute had gone all the Lego was put away.

When Mummy came in they were all smiling and happy; and when they saw the slipper that Mummy held in her right hand, they were very glad they had taken Jimmie's suggestion.

No glass between

This is a story of the long ago. It is true. The only thing I do not know about it is the little boy's real name. Let's call him Peter.

Peter lived in the poorest part of a big city. He was an orphan, his mother and father having died when he was very young. He was looked after by a lady who used to go to pubs and get drunk. Often she would smack him, and she never gave him enough to eat. His clothes were not mended. He had to go about with big holes in them – sometimes even in his trousers. His one pair of shoes was worn through. He looked very shabby and as if he needed someone to love him.

Peter never had any pocket money, and so he could never buy sweets or toys for himself; and certainly no one ever gave him any. His one great joy was to look into the toyshop windows at all the super things piled up inside. He knew he couldn't have them – for there was the glass between. Sometimes he would put his hands on the glass and try to imagine that he could touch the things on the other side.

There was one thing above all that he wanted – a box of toy soldiers. Often he would look through the glass at the brightly-coloured figures so neatly packed in their oblong boxes, or maybe standing

on the top of a castle. How he longed for just one soldier of his very own! But always there was the glass between, and home he had to go, unsatisfied.

Then one day Peter met with an accident. Crossing a road he tripped over a dog, and before he could get up a car ran over his leg. People crowded around, a policeman came up, and in a few minutes Peter was in an ambulance, being driven to the hospital. He woke up to find himself in a comfortable, snow-white bed, and to see a kind face bending over him. He thought he must be in heaven; it was all so different from what he had known before.

Some time later, when his leg began to get better, he was propped up in bed, and told that if he was a very good boy perhaps someone special would come to see him.

It was Christmas time, and in the afternoon several nurses came into the ward together with a lady who was dressed in beautiful clothes such as poor little Peter had never seen before. The lady began to give presents to all the children in their little white beds. Soon she came to where Peter was lying.

With a smile she handed a parcel to him. Peter said 'Thank you' very nicely. Eagerly he tore off the tissue paper.

There was a cry of delight. Everybody stopped and looked around.

'You seem very pleased', said the lady, with a broad smile.

'Oh!' cried Peter, 'it's a real box of soldiers, and there's no glass between!'

Those words of little Peter's made me think of some words just like them that we find in the Bible, where the apostle Paul says that now we see 'through a glass darkly', but afterward 'face to face'. I'm sure that what Paul meant was that while now we may not have all that we would like to have, and troubles come to us, and things are misunderstood, at the glorious time when Jesus comes again everything will be made clear and plain; all that is beautiful will be given to us, and there will be 'no glass between'.

Rover to the rescue

Jane was a lucky little girl. She had a beautiful big dog all of her very own. Rover had come to the house as a puppy when Jane was little, and the two had grown up together. They loved each other very much. Sometimes Jane would pretend Rover was sick. Then she would dress up as a nurse and try to give him medicine out of a bottle. But Rover was too wise for that. He didn't mind her tying him all up in bandages, but he did draw the line at taking medicine – unless it was something with plenty of sugar in it.

Rover was like Mary's little lamb. He followed Jane everywhere she went. If she went into town shopping for her mummy, Rover would go too. He even went to school with her, and it was the biggest job in the world to keep him out of the classroom. However, he was very obedient, and when Jane said 'No!' as though she really meant it, Rover would always do what he was told.

Then one night Rover disappeared. In the morning Jane went to his kennel as usual to give him his breakfast, but he was not there. All day she waited for him to come back, but he didn't return.

'Mummy,' she said at last, 'I must go and look for Rover. I'm sure he must be hungry by this time.'

But Mummy persuaded her to wait until the next

morning to see if he came back by then. But morning came again, and there was no sign of Rover. Then they both began to get worried, and asked the neighbours if they had seen Rover, even going to the police station, but they couldn't help.

When Jane reached home after school and heard that Rover had not returned, she made up her mind to go in search for him. She knew one place that Rover liked very much. She thought that he might have gone there and met with some accident. It was a wood a few miles out of town where there were many rabbits.

Jane was so determined to find her Rover that she had no fear of the woods or the lonely road. Bravely she walked on, calling 'Rover! Rover!' every now and then. But there was no response. No happy, barking Rover came bounding to answer her call. She began to get a little discouraged, and wondered whether it was really worth while going on. Then she decided that she would walk another three hundred steps and then turn back.

She began to count the steps, and in a little while passed one hundred, then two hundred, then three hundred. She was just turning to go home when, from somewhere on her right came a low cry as of someone in pain. Poor little Jane was quite frightened. Suddenly it occurred to her that she was all alone in the woods. No little girl – or little boy for that matter – should ever, ever, ever be alone. And never, never, never in the woods. Then the sound came again, a little different this time. A new idea came to Jane. She thought she had heard that noise before, sometimes in the middle of the night when Rover was lonely, or perhaps when he was trying to sing to the moon, as dogs sometimes do.

Again the sound came, this time a little more clearly. Jane now felt sure that it was Rover. It took a lot of courage to do it, but Jane was so determined to rescue her pet that she turned off the footpath and made her way through the trees in the direction from which the sound had come. That was very foolish of her and something she should not have done. As she went on, the cry became clearer and clearer until, at last, peering through some bushes she discovered Rover lying on the ground with his front paw caught in a steel trap!

'Oh, my poor, poor Rover!' she cried, kneeling down beside him. 'Somehow I must set you free.'

Jane had not seen a trap before, but she worked away at it until at last she had the teeth open wide enough to let poor Rover pull his foot out. Rover wanted to say how thankful he was, but he was too weak to give more than a faint wag of his tail. Jane had brought some biscuits with her in the hope of finding her pet. How glad he was for some food as he had not had any for two whole days!

Then there was the job of getting Rover home. He couldn't put his poor foot to the ground, and he

had to limp all the way back on three legs. It took them a long time, and Jane wished that she could carry Rover, but he was much too big for that. At last they reached home. In her delight at seeing Rover back again, Mummy forgot to scold Jane for going away all by herself. She said she thought Jane was a very brave little girl to go so far in search of her pet, but that she mustn't ever do it again without letting her know.

And now Jane had to be a real nurse to Rover. A vet came and put his leg in bandages and said it would be a week or two before he would walk properly again. So Jane gave him special care and all the food he liked best.

Rover never forgot Jane's kindness to him, and when he was well again he loved his little mistress more than ever. In his doggie way he seemed to try to show her how much he loved her. He never let her get far out of his sight.

One afternoon some months later, Jane took Rover with her for a walk by the river. He loved to go there, for there were so many things to chase! It was a very pretty walk that they had often taken together. Mother, of course, had told Jane that she must never leave the footpath, and it was only on this condition that she was allowed to go there. But somehow this time Jane forgot. She noticed some pretty flowers growing down by the water's edge, and thought it would be nice to pick a few and take them home. She felt sure Mummy wouldn't mind, especially when she saw the flowers. But the bank was slippery and much steeper than Jane had thought. Tripping over a tree root, she fell forward, rolling over and over, and splashed into the water. In a moment she was caught by the swiftly-flowing current and carried out into the stream.

'Help!' she screamed.

There was no one about; but Rover, who was sniffing around the field, heard her cry. He looked around, and seeing that Jane was no longer on the bank where he had left her, seemed to guess at once what had happened. Like a flash he bounded to the riverside. There was a spring and a splash, and a moment later Rover was swimming as hard as he could towards the struggling, spluttering figure of little Jane.

Now it was Rover's turn to help Jane. The brave dog put every ounce of his strength into the race to save his mistress. On and on he swam.

Just in time he reached her and caught her clothes in his teeth. Then came the hard struggle of swimming with her to the bank. But he did it, and as they were nearing the bank, Jane was able to catch hold of a tree stump, which helped them both to scramble out.

What happened when at last the two wet and soggy friends reached home you can imagine. When Mummy heard Jane's story she didn't know whether to scold, or to cry, or to laugh. She was so thankful that they had both come back safely.

Rover was given the most wonderful tea that evening, better than anything he could remember, or that he might have imagined in his most hungry moments. Jane and Rover remained the closest and best of friends for as long as he lived, and all the children around who heard of Rover's brave rescue, learned the lesson that kindness to animals is always rewarded.

Sticking pins in Billy

Young William Croker, known to the other boys in the town as 'Billy', was a very clever lad, but he had one fault. He thought so much of himself that his hat would hardly go on his head.

Billy was good at games. That made him a natural leader of the boys, but they all secretly disliked him because he was always boasting about the wonderful things he could do. He never had time to listen to what the other boys had to say, but would always interrupt them with a story of some experience he had had. If someone said he had seen a big frog, Billy would say, 'That's nothing; last week I saw one much bigger than that.'

At last the other boys became tired of his boasting, and began to talk over ways and means of putting an end to it. As Tommy Walters said, 'Billy is swollen up with pride as big as a balloon, and it's high time somebody stuck a pin in him.'

But how to do it was another question. Some of the boys suggested ducking him in the river; but Billy was quite a strong boy, and none of the others wanted to take the risk of having a quarrel with him. Then Tommy had a bright idea.

'I know of something better than that', he said. 'It wouldn't be kind to put him in the river, and it wouldn't do him much good anyhow. Have you ever thought what is the matter with Billy?'

The others crowded round. 'No, what?' they asked.

'I'll tell you. You've all noticed how Billy seems to win all our games', said Tommy. 'That's the trouble with him; he thinks we're no good, and that he can always beat us. If we are going to stop his boasting, we must learn to play better ourselves.'

'Good idea', said another boy. 'If we could make Billy lose every game for a few weeks, he would soon change his tune.'

'You're right,' said Tommy, 'but it's up to us to beat him. Why not practise some of our games on the quiet, and then surprise Billy?'

'But we can't all win', said a pale-faced, frightened boy; 'and I don't see how we can practise all the games we play.'

'No!' said Tommy. 'Of course we can't all practise everything at once. But let one or two practise running, some jumping, and others football.'

'Hurray!' laughed the others. 'Let's do it.'

Tommy's idea certainly put new life into those boys. Their mothers and teachers soon began to wonder what was the matter with them, for nearly all of them began to practise hard at the game they had chosen in their secret meeting.

Billy, too, noticed it but did not suspect that all this effort was directed against him. As the days went by he began to notice the results of the plan.

6
4
1

In running races he had been able to keep an easy lead but a few of the boys now began to keep up with him. Some passed him, and instead of always winning, he learned what it meant to lose.

When the school sports day came around, so many pins were stuck into Billy that he was reduced to almost normal size. Billy had not bothered to practise for any of the events because he felt so certain of success. The other boys, however, had worked very hard with one purpose in view, and they won. Poor Billy did not win a single race.

He felt bad about it, but was sure he would be able to do well in the game of cricket which was to follow the sports, because he prided himself on being a good batsman.

This game was always a big affair, at least in the boys' eyes, as it was held on a proper pitch and there were many people watching.

Billy was batting first. He told the boys that he was going to make at least fifty runs, and that they had better keep their eye on the town clock, because he was going to hit a ball right in the middle of it. Then, carrying his bat with a real swagger, he strolled across the field as though he were a professional. But Billy was caught for a duck!

In the next innings Tommy was batting first. He saw at once that his great opportunity had come. After all he had said to the other boys, he knew what he must do now.

Tommy had been practising batting and fielding every morning and evening. He walked onto the pitch sure he would score well. The bowler sent him a fast ball. But Tommy was ready; he had been training his eye carefully and he was sure of his strokes. He hit the ball. Billy could have caught it, he dropped it, and Tommy scored a run.

He scored more runs that day, partly because Billy, who was a really good player, lost his nerve at being beaten, and partly because he had worked so hard to succeed. Billy didn't make a single run.

At the end of the game they all crowded around Tommy and proclaimed him the hero of the day.

As for Billy, no one would have thought he was the same boy who had walked so confidently onto the pitch a couple of hours before.

'What about the town clock?' piped a small voice.

'And those fifty runs?' ventured a bolder voice.

But Billy only walked away with his head down. That was the last 'pin' that Billy needed to have stuck in him. No one ever heard him boasting again.

Elizabeth
Newton